Disney's

The Aristocats

Read *all* the Junior Novelizations
of Disney animated classics!

DISNEY'S

The Aristocats

Adapted from the film
by Cathy East Dubowski

DISNEY
PRESS

NEW YORK

First Edition

1 3 5 7 9 10 8 6 4 2

Library of Congress Catalog Card Number: 94-74639

ISBN: 0-7868-4053-6

Disney's
The Aristocats

CHAPTER ONE

Paris, 1930
Long ago in the beautiful city of Paris, a grand old mansion stood behind wrought-iron gates, surrounded by elegant gardens. Inside there lived a beautiful white cat named Duchess and her three kittens—Toulouse, Berlioz, and Marie.

What lucky cats they were! Paris was filled with ordinary cats, strays who prowled through garbage bins for scraps to eat, who slept in doorways and cold back alleys. But

Duchess and her children dined on the finest cream served in polished silver dishes. At night they slept in a luxurious cat bed near a cozy fire.

They were, in fact, Aristocats—well bred, well fed, and living in the lap of luxury.

Ah, but that is not why we are so lucky, Duchess thought one day as she rode through the streets of Paris in a fine horse-drawn carriage. On the seat beside her lay a pile of packages from the city's finest shops. Of course she was grateful for all the material gifts her children received. But she knew that her family's true wealth did not lie in any of these beautiful things.

Duchess purred as a gentle jeweled hand stroked her fur. She looked up into a face still beautiful though lined with age. The eyes had not lost their sparkle, the lips still offered the world a smile.

Ah, *oui*, we are lucky, Duchess thought, because we live with Madame Adelaide Bonfamille. We are lucky because she is kind and gentle. We are lucky because she loves us.

And no one could put a price tag on that.

The carriage passed through the wrought-iron gates and stopped before the mansion's front door. Edgar the butler hurried out and helped Madame as she stepped gracefully from the carriage. Behind her, head held high, Duchess stepped down just as gracefully.

"Thank you, Edgar," Madame said. Her arms full of packages, she strode toward the front door.

But then she stopped. With a smile, Madame turned back to the horse who pulled her carriage. "Of course, Frou-Frou, I almost forgot." She held out her hand.

Frou-Frou whinnied. Sugar cubes! Madame never forgot the faithful horse's favorite treat.

Edgar reached for Madame's packages. "May I take these for you, Madame? They really are much too heavy for you—"

"*Tut, tut,* Edgar," Madame said. "Don't fuss over me."

Edgar rushed ahead and held open the front door. Madame paused on the doorstep. "Come along, Duchess, kittens."

She entered the house, then stuck her head back out, her eyes shining brightly. "Oh, and Edgar, I'm expecting my attorney this morning. You remember him, of course?"

"Of course, Madame," Edgar said politely. But as Madame Bonfamille hurried inside, the butler sighed and rolled his eyes. "How could anyone forget him?"

A short while later, a newfangled automobile chugged up in front of Madame's house. A very old but very dapper white-haired gentleman wearing a black top hat cut the motor and flung open the door. He was singing loudly as he jumped from the car: *"Ta-ra-ra-BOOM-de-aye, ta-ra-ra-BOOM-de-aye. . . ."* But when his polished boots hit the stone sidewalk, he nearly fell down.

"Whoops!" The gentleman steadied himself with his cane and chuckled. "I guess I'm not as spry as I was at eighty," he muttered.

Humming, he scooted up the walk and knocked.

Edgar opened the door. "Good day, sir," he said with a crisp bow. "Madame is expecting you."

The gentleman whistled as he strolled into the marble hall. He tipped his cane to his top hat and flipped it into the air.

It landed squarely on Edgar's head.

Edgar pursed his lips. "Another ringer, sir. You never miss."

The gentleman cackled and charged for the stairs. "Come on, Edgar. The last one up is a nincompoop!"

Here we go again, Edgar thought with a sigh. "Couldn't we take the elevator, sir?"

"That birdcage?" exclaimed the gentleman. "Poppycock! Elevators are for old people." He tried to take the stairs two at a time, but his legs seemed to have forgotten how.

Edgar caught the lawyer just as he toppled backward. "May I give you a hand, sir?"

The gentleman jabbed Edgar in the ribs. "You haven't got an extra foot, have you?"

Edgar sighed patiently. "That always makes me laugh, sir. Every time."

With a shout of laughter, the lawyer jumped onto Edgar's back as if going for a horseback ride. "Upward and onward, Edgar! *Wheeee!*"

With a groan, Edgar carried the playful

old man the rest of the way up the stairs.

At the end of the upstairs hall the white-haired gentleman slid from Edgar's shoulders as the butler knocked at Madame's door.

"Come in," Madame called from within.

When Edgar opened the door, Madame stood in the center of the room with Duchess in her arms. The three kittens were playing nearby. Madame smoothed her dress and touched her hand to her elegantly styled white hair as the two men entered. Her cheeks flushed pink as she smiled at her guest.

The old gentleman straightened his cravat and the flower in his lapel and smiled back.

Edgar cleared his throat: "Announcing Monsieur Georges Hautecourt—"

"Oh, my goodness, Edgar," Madame said with a wave of her hand. "I know Georges."

Indeed, Madame Bonfamille and Monsieur Hautecourt had been the best of friends for many, many years.

Monsieur Hautecourt rushed past Edgar with an eager smile. "Adelaide . . . my dear."

Madame held Duchess in one arm as she held out her right hand.

But poor Monsieur Hautecourt had grown very nearsighted. Instead of kissing Madame's hand, he bent and kissed Duchess's fluffy white tail!

"Ah," murmured Monsieur Hautecourt. "You still have the softest hands in all of Paris, my dear."

Madame's laughter tinkled like wind chimes in a spring breeze. "Oh, Georges, you are such a flirt."

Duchess and her kittens watched happily. They loved it when Monsieur Hautecourt came to call. He always brought good times and laughter to Madame's quiet mansion.

Berlioz, the most musically inclined of the three kittens, jumped to the table and wound up the gramophone. The turntable began to spin, and Berlioz set the needle down on the record. Music floated across the room.

"Adelaide!" cried Monsieur Hautecourt. "That music! It's from *Carmen*, isn't it?"

"That's right. It was my favorite role."

"It was the night of your grand premiere that we first met. Remember? How we celebrated your success! Champagne, dancing the night away . . ."

Monsieur Hautecourt seized Madame's hands and twirled her around the room—with Duchess sandwiched in between.

Marie and Toulouse danced playfully around their feet.

At last Madame gasped for breath and sank down onto the velvet love seat, hugging Duchess to her cheek. "Oh, Georges. We're just a pair of sentimental old fools."

Monsieur Hautecourt kept dancing around the room as if he might never stop.

"Come, now, Georges," Madame said with a fond smile. "Do be serious."

Monsieur Hautecourt danced over to his briefcase and waltzed it over to a little desk in one corner of the room. He spread out his papers and pen and bottle of ink, then turned to Madame. "Yes?"

"I've asked you to come here on a very important legal matter," she said.

"Splendid!" exclaimed Monsieur Hautecourt. "Whom do you want me to sue?"

"Oh, come now, Georges," Madame said,

laughing. "I don't wish to sue anyone. I simply want to make my will."

"Ah, yes," Monsieur Hautecourt said with a quiet smile. He put on his spectacles and dipped his pen into the ink. "Now then, to whom do you wish to leave your fortune?"

Madame smiled a little wistfully as she stroked Duchess's white fur. "As you know, I have no living relatives. And naturally I want my beloved cats to always be well cared for. And certainly no one can do this better than my faithful servant, Edgar. . . . "

Down in the servants' quarters, Edgar the butler was ironing his pants. But he could hear every word Madame and Monsieur were saying. A brass listening pipe ran from Madame's room to his. It had been installed so Madame could call Edgar when she needed him.

But it also worked well for eavesdropping.

Hearing his own name, Edgar leaned closer to the pipe.

"Edgar?" he heard Monsieur Hautecourt exclaim. "Adelaide! You mean to say you're leaving your vast fortune to Edgar, your butler? Everything you possess . . . stocks, bonds, this mansion . . . your country château?"

Downstairs, a huge smile broke out on Edgar's face. Could it be true?

Edgar's smile grew wider as Monsieur Hautecourt continued: "Art treasures, jewels . . ."

Edgar began to dance with joy. At last all his years of faithful service to Madame were going to pay off—literally!

"No, no, Georges," Madame said.

Edgar stopped in mid-twirl.

"I'm leaving everything to my cats!" Madame announced.

"To your cats?" Monsieur Hautecourt asked.

"To her *cats*!" Edgar exclaimed.

"Yes, Georges," Madame said, unaware that her butler was listening. "I simply wish to have the cats inherit my fortune first. Then, at the end of their life span, my entire estate will pass on to Edgar."

Edgar didn't hear any more. He plopped down on his trunk in amazement. "Her cats inherit first?" he exclaimed. "And *I* come *after* the cats? Oh, it's not fair! After all I've done for her!"

He got up and began to pace his small room. "Each cat will live about twelve years," he mumbled, counting on his fingers. Then his face went pale. "But each cat has nine lives! That's four times twelve, and multiply that by nine times . . . I'll never live that long! I'll be dead and gone before I get my hands on a single coin."

Edgar slowly pulled his pants off the ironing board, thinking hard. He couldn't let this happen. He had served Madame night and day. He had put up with that nutty lawyer and those fussy cats for years. He deserved to be rewarded. But what could he do?

Edgar's face twisted into an evil grin as a black thought filled his heart. "I'll just think up a way to get rid of them!" He chuckled wickedly. "There are a *million* reasons why I should—all of them dollars!"

He yanked on his pants so hard, they ripped.

Scowling, he laid his pants on the iron-ing board and went to search for a needle and thread. "Those cats," he muttered. "Those cats have got to go!"

CHAPTER TWO

"Wait for me! Wait for me!" Berlioz ran up the front steps of Madame's house the next day, trying to catch up with his brother and sister.

Toulouse dived for the kitty door. It was a special swinging entrance at the bottom of the mansion's regular front door. There was one at the back door as well. It allowed the cats to come and go as they pleased, so they never had to scratch and meow for Edgar to let them in.

"Me first! Me first!" Marie cried.

All three kittens tried to squeeze through the kitty door at once.

"Why should you be first?" Toulouse asked.

"Because I'm a lady!" said Marie haughtily.

"You're not a lady," snapped Toulouse. "You're nothin' but a sister!"

Marie finally popped through and jumped down onto the polished marble floor. But Berlioz grabbed her tail and yanked her back so he could run ahead.

The kittens chased one another around the house, from one antique chair to the next, around fragile lamps and statuettes, in and out of the velvet drapes.

At last Berlioz jumped on Marie and began to tickle her.

"Get her, Berlioz, get her!" Toulouse cheered.

But Marie rolled out from under him and yanked on the red ribbon around Berlioz's neck.

"Hey," cried Berlioz, "fight fair!"

"I'll help you!" Toulouse cried. Meowing a battle cry, he leaped onto a table just above the fight, knocking over a candleholder. The candle fell and broke in two on Marie's head.

"Ouch! That hurts!" cried Marie. "Mama! Mama!"

Duchess hurried in and stared at her kittens in amazement. "Children!"

Toulouse, Berlioz, and Marie froze at the sound of their mother's voice.

"Marie, darling, you must stop," said Duchess. "This is really not ladylike. And Berlioz! Such behavior is most unbecoming to a gentleman."

"Well, she started it," Berlioz grumbled.

"Ladies do not start fights," Marie said tilting her little pink nose into the air. Then she shook her paw at her brother. "But they sure can finish 'em!"

Berlioz stuck out his tongue.

"Berlioz!" his mother cried. "Don't be rude."

"But, Mama," he said. "We were just practicing biting and clawing."

With a sigh Duchess sat down and gathered her children around her. "Aristocats do *not* practice biting and clawing."

"But, Mama," Toulouse said. "Someday we might meet a tough alley cat." He swatted his paws at an imaginary cat. *"Fffft! Fffft!"* he hissed, arching his back and fluffing out his tail.

Duchess laughed at Toulouse in spite of herself. "That will do, young man. Come. It's time we concerned ourselves with self-improvement. You want to grow up to be charming ladies and gentlemen, don't you?"

Duchess sent Berlioz to the piano to practice his scales while Marie practiced her singing.

"Now, Toulouse," Duchess said. "Go and start with your painting."

Toulouse scampered over to his easel. Even at his age, he was a very talented painter . . . but a bit messy. He pounced on his tubes of paint, and colors squirted everywhere. He never used a brush. He mixed the paint with his paws, then smeared it across the canvas. Some of it splattered onto the wall and dripped down a portrait of a stern-faced Edgar.

"Uh-oh! Old Pickle Puss Edgar won't like that!" Toulouse snickered.

Berlioz and Marie howled with laughter. Duchess had to bite her tongue to keep from giggling. She had to admit, Edgar the butler did have a rather sour disposition. But of course, it was not polite to call him names. "Now, Berlioz!" said Duchess. "That is not kind. You know Edgar is so fond of us all. And he takes very good care of us. . . ."

Downstairs, in the mansion's well-equipped kitchen, that is exactly what Edgar the butler was planning to do—take care of the cats for good! He hummed happily as he warmed some heavy cream in a saucepan on the cast-iron stove.

Now for that extra ingredient. . . . Edgar glanced over his shoulder to make sure he was alone. Then he sneaked a glass bottle from his coat pocket. He had purchased the bottle at the chemist's the evening before. The label read SLEEPING PILLS.

Slowly Edgar poured the pills—every single one of them—into the saucepan of cream. He stirred gently to make sure all the pills completely dissolved. As he stirred he sang softly, "Rock-a-bye, kitties, bye-bye you go. *La, la, la, la,* and I'm in the dough. . . ."

Edgar giggled as he searched the shelves

for some additional seasonings. "Oh, Edgar, you sly old fox!" he whispered to himself.

Then he added a pinch of this and a dash of that. He wanted to make sure this dish was absolutely delicious so that Duchess and her kittens would drink up every last drop.

CHAPTER THREE

The moment arrived. Dinnertime! Edgar
climbed the stairs with a cloth-covered silver
tray in his hands. As he reached the landing,
he scowled at the noise that assaulted his
ears. That little beast Marie was screeching as
Berlioz pounced up and down on the key-
board of Madame's grand piano. How foolish
of Madame to allow those cats to play on such
a fine instrument, Edgar thought. But then he
smiled. For if his plan worked well, the
piano—and everything else in the mansion—

would soon belong to him.

Edgar tapped on the door and entered with the cats' special dinner. "Ah, good evening, my little ones," he murmured with fake affection. "Your favorite dish . . . prepared in a very special way."

Berlioz, Toulouse, and Marie hurried over with hungry meows as Edgar set the tray on the floor. He whisked away the cloth to reveal four steaming bowls. "Crème de la crème à la Edgar," he announced.

The butler nearly shouted with joy as he watched the kittens lap up the cream. "Sleep well—oh! I-I mean, *eat*! Eat well," he sputtered. With his face turning a deep scarlet, he hurried out the door.

The room was quiet as the hungry cats ate their meal. Duchess insisted on good manners, even when they had no company.

Across the room a tiny gray mouse poked his nose out of his hole and sniffed. Shyly he crept out with a huge cracker tucked under his arm. No one noticed the quiet little mouse at first, so he cleared his throat. "*Ahem.* Good evening, Duchess."

Duchess looked up and smiled. "Good

evening, Monsieur Roquefort." The little mouse was a friend of the family's—for Aristocats *never* ate mice.

"*Hmmm,*" said Roquefort. "Something smells awfully good. What is that wonderful smell?"

Marie wiped her mouth with the back of her paw. "It's crème de la crème à la Edgar."

"Won't you join us, Monsieur Roquefort?" Duchess said.

"Yes!" Roquefort squeaked. "I mean, thank you. It just so happens I have a cracker with me."

He scampered up and dunked his cracker into the warm cream. He took a bite and sighed in delight. "Ummm. *Very* good. My compliments to the chef!" He devoured the entire cream-soaked cracker in a few quick bites. "In fact," he added, smacking his lips, "this calls for another cracker!"

Roquefort ran back toward his house. Halfway there he began to yawn. Two steps away his eyes drooped closed. By the time he reached the wall, he stumbled and fell head-first into his hole.

Roquefort was fast asleep.

A few minutes later Duchess yawned politely behind her paw and glanced around. How curious, she thought. Roquefort never returned for his second helping of this delicious dinner. Perhaps the little mouse's eyes were bigger than his stomach tonight, she thought with a smile.

Yawning again, Duchess urged her sleepy-eyed children to clean their plates. Many a cat would go hungry in the city of Paris tonight, she reminded them. They were lucky to have such a delicious meal prepared especially for them.

CHAPTER FOUR

The sky was like black velvet, the stars like glittering diamonds over the sleeping city of Paris that night. The many rooms of Madame's mansion were silent except for the old grandfather clock that gently chimed the late hour.

And then . . . footsteps. Someone was tiptoeing through the mansion.

The small kitty door at the back of the house opened with a soft, slow *S-C-R-E-E-C-H*.

But it wasn't a cat who peeked out. It was Edgar the butler. His eyes darted left and right. Not a soul was in sight. Good! He slipped back inside, and the kitty door swung shut with a soft *thwack!*

Seconds later the doorknob turned. Edgar stepped out into the chilly night air, a large wicker basket in his hands. Squinting into the darkness, he tiptoed out . . .

And tripped over a garbage can.

Startled, he backed up. Someone jabbed a weapon of some kind into his back. Edgar's hands shot up in the air.

He stood there trembling for a moment. But when nothing happened and no one spoke, he slowly turned around.

Whew! thought Edgar, mopping the sweat from his brow. It was only a tree branch. Chuckling, he lugged the heavy basket over to his motorbike and dumped it into the sidecar.

Edgar straddled the seat, then lifted the basket's cover to peek inside.

There lay Duchess and her three kittens, fast asleep. Edgar grinned. The sleeping pills had worked like magic!

Toulouse stirred and struggled to open one eye. "Edgar . . ." he whispered. But he could not fight the powerful effect of the sleeping pills. Snoring softly, he snuggled up against his mother and sank back into a deep sleep as Edgar replaced the cover.

A wisp of cloud floated across the moon as Edgar drove away through the empty streets of Paris. He held his breath as he passed the police station. But no one paid attention to the quiet *putt-putt* of the motorbike.

The air grew colder as Edgar left the city streets behind and drove out into the peaceful French countryside. The sound of his motorbike woke up two farm dogs who had been sleeping beneath the stars.

"Hey, Lafayette," one of the dogs whispered from beneath a hay wagon. "Listen! Wheels approaching."

Lafayette poked his sleepy head out of a nearby pile of hay. "Oh, Napoleon!" he complained. "We already bit six tires today, chased four motorcars—plus a bicycle and a scooter."

"Hush your mouth!" Napoleon hissed.

31

He lifted his ear to the wind and listened. "It's a motorbike. One squeaky wheel—on the front, it sounds like."

Napoleon was wide awake now. There was nothing he enjoyed better than a good chase, no matter what time of day or night. Especially when there were wheels involved.

"Now, you go for the tires," he told Lafayette, "and I'll go right for the seat of the problem."

"How come you always get the tender parts?" Lafayette grumbled as he crawled out of the hay.

"Because I outrank you!" Napoleon snapped. "Ready? Here we go. *CHARGE!*"

Barking fiercely, the two dogs dashed under the fence and out into the lane—right in front of Edgar's motorbike.

Edgar shrieked and instantly yanked the steering wheel to the right. The motorbike skidded off the road. As it plunged toward the river, the basket of cats flew out of the bouncing sidecar and tumbled down the hill.

Edgar hung on for dear life as his motorbike splashed across the shallow river. As he churned up the bank on the other side, he

Madame Adelaide Bonfamille takes her beloved Aristocats for a ride.
Her butler, Edgar, drives Frou-Frou, the carriage horse.

Aging—but still dashing—Monsieur Georges Hautecourt sweeps
Madame off her feet to music from her favorite opera, *Carmen*.

Ladies first! But Berlioz and Toulouse certainly don't agree.

Napoleon and Lafayette prepare to charge off after the intruder, Edgar.

Duchess and her kittens, abandoned in the countryside, wonder how they will get back to Paris.

J. Thomas O'Malley, the alley cat, sweet-talks the elegant Duchess.

All aboard! O'Malley finagles a "magic carpet ride" straight to Paris.

O'Malley to the rescue!

The cats follow the Gabble sisters, Amelia and Abigail, back to Paris.

Scat Cat and his band jazz it up at O'Malley's bachelor pad.

O'Malley and Duchess spend a romantic evening on a moonlit rooftop in Paris.

Roquefort warns O'Malley that Edgar has nabbed Duchess and the kittens again!

Scat Cat and his band keep their claws in Edgar and watch as Frou-Frou prepares to kick!

It's O'Malley to the rescue again, as he frees Duchess and the kittens.

O'Malley, Duchess, and the kittens pose for their first family portrait.

could feel the two dogs' snapping jaws just inches behind him. Terrified, he roared up onto the road and raced back toward Paris without ever looking back.

CHAPTER FIVE

Thunder rumbled angrily across the midnight sky. Duchess woke up with a start. Her head felt groggy. She was cold and wet. And it was very, very dark.

She glanced around. "Where am I?" she whispered. "Why, I'm not at home at all."

But that was not the worst of it. Her precious children were gone!

Duchess frantically searched the darkness around her. "Children!" she called out.

"Berlioz! Toulouse! Marie! Where are you?"

At first only rumbles of thunder answered her call. But then she heard a frightened meow.

"Here I am, Mama!"

Duchess glanced up. Marie was caught in the branches of a tree. Quickly Duchess rescued her and set her gently on the ground. "Marie, darling. Are you all right?"

Marie yawned. "I guess I had a nightmare and fell out of bed."

Suddenly they heard Berlioz shouting: "Mama! Mama!" It came from behind some bushes.

Duchess and Marie hurried toward the sound. A very wet Berlioz crawled from the edge of the stream. A monster was chasing him—a scary, scaly monster that croaked! "Mama, help!" Berlioz cried.

"Now, now, darling," Duchess reassured him as he cowered behind her. "That's only a little frog, my love." Her city-born son had never seen a frog before.

"Now," she said when she was sure Berlioz and Marie were all right. "You two stay here while I look for Toulouse."

Duchess began to search for her missing kitten. "Toulouse!" she cried. "Toulouse! Where are you?"

"Toulouse! Toulouse!" cried Berlioz and Marie.

Suddenly the blanket over the basket twitched. Toulouse poked his nose out. "Hey— what's all the yellin' about?" he asked sleepily.

"Mama," called Marie. "He's been here all the time."

"Oh, thank goodness," said Duchess. She hurried over to lick her son's face. "Are you all right?"

Toulouse tumbled out of the basket, rubbing his eyes. "I was having this funny dream, Mama. Edgar was in it, and we were all bouncing along—"

"CROAK!"

Toulouse stared wide-eyed at the big bullfrog. "Uh-oh. It wasn't a dream!" He stared into his mother's worried face. "Mama! Edgar did this to us!"

"Edgar? Madame's butler?" Duchess exclaimed. "Oh, darling, why, that's ridiculous."

Just then thunder rumbled across the sky. The kittens glanced up and shivered.

They had never been outside in a storm before.

"Mama, I'm afraid," Marie cried. "I want to go home."

"Don't be frightened, dear," Duchess said. "Everything is going to be all right." She just hoped it was true.

A raindrop struck her on the nose. Then it began to pour.

"Quickly, children," Duchess instructed the kittens. "Into the basket."

Duchess moved the basket under the bridge. It wouldn't completely protect them from the rain, but it would help. She nudged her kittens into the basket and pulled the cover over their heads.

"What's going to happen to us?" Toulouse whispered.

"I wish we were home with Madame right now," Berlioz whimpered.

Marie just sniffled as she cuddled up against her brothers.

Duchess sighed. "Poor Madame. She'll be so worried when she finds us gone."

Miles away in Paris lightning flashed, illuminating the many rooms of Madame Bonfamille's silent mansion.

Madame sat up in her warm, dry bed, rubbing her temples. "Duchess . . . " she murmured, "kittens . . . Oh, my gracious. I had the most horrible dream about them."

Thunder rumbled through the room like an angry dog. Quickly Madame rose from her bed and slid her feet into her slippers. "Oh, dear, what a terrible night!" she said as she pulled on her robe and hurried to the blue-canopied cat bed by the window. "Now, now, my darlings, don't be frightened," she said as she knelt by the bed. "The storm will soon pass."

Just then another flash of lightning flooded the room with light. Madame gasped. The cat bed was empty.

"They're gone!" she cried. She rushed into the hallway. "Duchess! Kittens! Where are you?"

Madame kept calling out their names as she searched room after room. Empty! All of them, empty!

Now Madame was truly frightened. Duchess and her kittens were so well behaved, they never wandered the house at night. And they always came when she called.

Madame's heart sank. "They're gone," she whispered. "They're gone!"

A sleepy gray mouse poked his head out of his hole in the wall. "Duchess and her kittens . . . gone?"

He crawled up the draperies to peer out the rain-spattered window. "But where?" he wondered. "Why? Good heavens, anything could happen to them on a night like this. They could get washed down a storm drain, struck by lightning. . . ." Roquefort ran back to his hole to get his hat and coat. "I've got to find them!"

Moments later the little gray mouse pushed his way out through the kitty door. Big fat raindrops soaked him to the skin as he stood on the front porch.

Roquefort hesitated. He was only a tiny mouse. And the Paris that lay before him was a huge crowded city, full of danger. Duchess and her kittens could be anywhere.

But Duchess and her kittens had always been kind to him. That was something he could never forget. Bravely he marched off into the rain-drenched streets. "Duuuu-chess! Kiii-ttens!" he squeaked into the darkness. He would not give up until he found them.

CHAPTER SIX

Duchess awoke to the sound of singing.

She was curled up on the grass beside the basket where her children still slept. She stretched in the warm morning sunshine, a little sore from sleeping on the hard ground, but happy that the storm had passed and that her children were safe beside her.

But who *was* that singing?

Curious, Duchess crept out from beneath the bridge to look. A rather handsome cinnamon-colored alley cat was prancing back and forth in front of the river, admiring his reflection. Singing at the top of his lungs, he leaped up onto the railing of the bridge, danced a few steps, then froze when he spotted Duchess watching him.

He smiled flirtatiously and jumped into the tree above her. Still singing, he tapped the tree's blossoms, showering Duchess with fragrant pink petals. Then he introduced himself. "I'm Abraham de Lacy Giuseppe Casey Thomas O'Malley the Alley Cat," he exclaimed.

Duchess laughed merrily as she brushed the petals from her white fur. "Bravo!" she said, clapping her paws at his singing. "Very good. You are a great talent."

"Thank you," O'Malley said with a bow.

"Monsieur, your name seems to cover all of Europe."

"That's me!" he said with a wink. "I'm one of a kind. King of the highway, prince of the boulevard." He jumped to the ground beside her. "And what might your name be?"

"My name is Duchess," she said shyly.

"Duchess," O'Malley repeated in a whisper. "Beautiful. Love it. And those eyes! Why, your eyes are like sapphires, sparkling so bright, they make the morning radiant and light."

"*C'est très jolie,* Monsieur O'Malley," Duchess said, blushing. She looked at him shyly from beneath her lashes. What a rascal! she thought. And yet she found him rather charming.

Unseen by Duchess and O'Malley, the kittens peeked out of the basket.

"How romantic," Marie whispered.

"Sissy stuff!" Berlioz muttered with a scowl.

"Oh, boy," said Toulouse. "An alley cat!"

Duchess sighed, remembering her situation. "Mr. O'Malley, I'm afraid I'm really in a great deal of trouble."

"Trouble?" O'Malley said. "Hey, helping beautiful dames—ah, *damsels* in distress is my specialty. So what's the problem, Your Ladyship?"

"It is most important that I get back to Paris," Duchess explained. "So if you would just be so kind as to show me the way—"

"Show you the way?" O'Malley exclaimed. He snuggled up closer to this

43

beautiful high-class cat. "Why, darling, we shall fly to Paris on a magic carpet, side by side . . . just we two."

"Oh!" Marie cried, jumping out of the basket in excitement. "That would be wonderful!"

O'Malley stopped short and stared at the little white kitten. "Er—just we three?"

Berlioz and Toulouse jumped out of the basket and joined them.

O'Malley gulped. "Four? Five?"

"Oh, yes, Monsieur O'Malley," Duchess purred. "These are my children."

"How sweet," O'Malley said through gritted teeth.

The kittens crowded around him with eager faces.

"Do you *really* have a magic carpet?" Berlioz demanded.

"Are we *really* going to ride on it?" Marie asked.

"Well, uh," O'Malley stammered, "what I meant was . . ."

O'Malley was at a loss for words. When he'd spotted the beautiful Duchess, he'd had something a little more romantic in mind, a magic carpet built for two. A basketful of kittens was not part of his plans.

Duchess saw the change in O'Malley's expression, and she understood exactly. This handsome charmer was not really interested in helping them out at all.

"No poetry to cover this situation, Monsieur O'Malley?" she asked tartly.

When O'Malley didn't answer, Duchess nodded politely, then called to her kittens as she walked toward the road, "Come, children." This road must lead somewhere, Duchess thought. She would just have to give it a try. Somehow she would find the way back to Paris.

O'Malley watched the proud Duchess and her well-behaved kittens march single file toward the dusty country road. He was pretty sure by the looks of them that a life on the road was not at all what they were used to. He had to admit, that Duchess dame had a lot of guts.

"That's quite a family," O'Malley mumbled to himself. "And you know what, O'Malley? You're not a cat—you're a *rat*!"

He ran to catch up with them. "Hey, wait up!"

Duchess stopped and stared at him coolly. But the kittens' faces filled with hope.

"Now, look, kids," O'Malley told them, "if I said magic carpet, magic carpet it's gonna be. And it's gonna stop for passengers right . . . here." He drew an X in the dirt with his claw.

"Oh boy!" Berlioz cried. "We're going to fly after all!"

"Now," O'Malley said, pointing to the bushes by the side of the road, "hide over there. And you just leave the rest to J. Thomas O'Malley." Then he leaped into a nearby tree.

Duchess was still a little suspicious of O'Malley's motives, but she allowed the kittens to drag her into the bushes with them. O'Malley perched on a branch of the tree and waited.

Soon the cats heard the roar of an engine approaching. Duchess and her kittens peeked out through the bushes. A milk truck was rumbling down the road.

"One magic carpet comin' up!" O'Malley

crowed.

"*That's* a magic carpet?" Duchess whispered skeptically.

The truck rumbled toward the tree. At precisely the perfect second O'Malley jumped—

And landed on the hood of the car. *"MEOWWRRRLLL!"*

"Sacré bleu!" the milkman shrieked, slamming on the brakes. The truck kicked up a shower of dirt and gravel as it skidded, then choked to a stop.

The man got out and shook his fist. "Stupid cat!" he shouted. "Brainless lunatic!" He stomped around to the front of the truck. Now he would have to crank up the engine to start the truck's motor again.

At the back of the truck O'Malley stood grinning by the **X** he had scratched in the dirt. "All right, step lively," he called. "All aboard for Paris!"

"Why, Monsieur O'Malley," Duchess exclaimed. "You could have lost your life!"

O'Malley shrugged. "So, I got a few to spare."

Duchess helped her kittens jump into

the back of the truck. "How can we ever thank you?" she asked, looking down at O'Malley.

"My pleasure entirely," O'Malley said. He blew her a kiss. "*Aloha. Bon soir. Sayonara* and all those good-byes, baby."

Marie waved as the truck pulled away. "*Sayonara*—oh!"

The truck had just hit a bump in the road. Marie lost her balance and tumbled from the back of the truck.

"*Mama!*"

"Marie!" Duchess cried.

In a flash O'Malley had scooped Marie up and leaped onto the back of the truck.

Duchess reached out for her kitten and hugged her tightly.

"Haven't we met before?" O'Malley joked.

"Yes," Duchess said with a warm smile. "And I'm so glad we did."

"Oh, Monsieur O'Malley," Marie exclaimed. "Thank you for saving my life!"

"No trouble at all, little princess." O'Malley grinned at the three kittens. "And when we get to Paris, I'll show you all the time of your life."

"Oh, but we just couldn't," Duchess said. "You see, my mistress will be so worried about us."

O'Malley snorted. "Well, humans don't really worry too much about their pets."

"Oh, no, you just don't understand," Duchess insisted. "Madame loves us very much. She says we are her greatest treasure."

"Yeah, right," O'Malley muttered. He didn't trust humans—any of them. That's why he lived a life on the road, footloose and free as the wind, with no human to tell him what to do and when. But he agreed to help Duchess and her family find their way home to this human they called Madame.

After all, he thought, throwing Duchess another long look, how could he say no to those beautiful sapphire eyes?

Back in Paris, Frou-Frou whinnied and paced in her stall. She stopped only when a little gray mouse shuffled into the barn.

"Oh, Roquefort!" the horse exclaimed in

relief. "I've been so worried about you. Did you find them?"

Roquefort shook his head sadly. "Not a sign of them, Frou-Frou. And I've searched all night."

"Poor Madame didn't sleep a wink."

"It's a sad day for all of us," Roquefort agreed.

Suddenly their gloom was broken by a cheerful sound. They heard Edgar the butler coming toward the barn. And he was humming!

"Good morning, Frou-Frou, my pretty horse," Edgar called out happily. "Can you keep a secret?" He laughed. "Of course you can." After all, he knew very well that animals couldn't talk!

Edgar held up the morning newspaper. "Look, Frou-Frou. I've made the headlines!" The headline read:

MYSTERIOUS KIDNAPPER ABDUCTS FAMILY OF CATS

"So he's the catnapper!" Roquefort squeaked.

Edgar patted Frou-Frou on the head.

"Aren't you proud of me? The police said it was a masterful professional job. The work of a genius. Not bad, eh?"

Frou-Frou whinnied angrily.

Edgar began to feed the horse her morning oats. "Oh, they won't find a clue to link it to me. Not one single clue. Why, if they do, I'll eat my hat."

CHAPTER SEVEN

"Anyone for breakfast?" O'Malley asked.

"Breakfast?" Toulouse asked. "Where?"

O'Malley patted an odd canvas-covered shape in the back of the truck. "Why, right here under this magic carpet. But first," he added, "we have to cook up a little magic."

The kittens stared, breathless.

"First wiggle your nose and tickle your chin," O'Malley instructed.

The kittens wiggled their noses and tickled their chins.

"Then," O'Malley continued, "close your eyes and cross your heart . . ."

The kittens obediently closed their eyes and crossed their hearts.

O'Malley whisked the canvas cover away. "Presto!"

The kittens opened their eyes. There, right in front of them, stood several large metal cans. The one in front was marked CREAM.

"*Hurray!*" shouted Marie.

"We did it!" Berlioz cheered.

O'Malley yanked off the lid. The kittens jumped onto the top edge of the can and began to lap up the cream.

Duchess shook her head in admiration. "Why, Monsieur O'Malley. You are amazing."

O'Malley grinned. "True, true."

But now, up on top of the milk cans, the kittens could be seen through the small window in the cab of the truck. The grouchy driver glanced in his rearview mirror. Cats? In the cream? *"Sacré bleu!"* he cried and slammed on the brakes once more.

The frightened cats leaped from the back of the truck just in the nick of time.

The driver hobbled to the edge of the road and shook both fists at the fleeing hitchhikers. "Thieves!" he shouted. "Robbers!" In a rage he grabbed things from the back of the truck and began to throw them at the cats.

A heavy metal wrench whizzed past Toulouse's ear. A bucket almost hit Marie.

"Take that, you mangy tramps!" the milkman shouted.

The cats ran and ran until the man's angry shouts faded behind them. At last they stopped to catch their breath.

Duchess checked each kitten to make sure they were all safe. "What a horrible, horrible man!"

"Well," said O'Malley, "some humans are like that, Duchess. I've learned to live with them."

"I'll show him!" Toulouse growled. He arched his back and bared his claws. *"Fffft! Fffft!"* he hissed.

"Hey, watch out, little tiger," O'Malley teased with a chuckle. The kid actually reminded him a little of himself at that age.

"I'll be so glad when we get back home," Duchess said.

"Well, it's a long way off," O'Malley said. "So we'd better get moving." He led them to some railroad tracks. They could follow them toward Paris.

The kittens ran ahead.

"Let's play train," Toulouse suggested.

Toulouse pretended to be the engine, Berlioz stood in for the middle car, and Marie chugged behind as the caboose.

"Choo, choo, choo, choo—whooo-whooo!" Toulouse shouted as the kittens marched onto a railroad bridge that arched high above a wide river.

"Children, be careful!" Duchess called. She and O'Malley followed them onto the bridge.

"Clickety-clack, clickety-clack, whooo-whooo!" Toulouse cried.

Tooot-toooooooot!

Everyone jumped. That wasn't Toulouse. It was a real whistle—a train was coming. The cats were right in the middle of the bridge. There was no way they could make it to the other side before the speeding train reached them.

"Don't panic!" O'Malley ordered. "Get down—here, beneath the tracks."

O'Malley quickly showed Duchess and the kittens how to hide on the wooden trestle beneath the metal tracks.

Tooot-toooooooot!

The bridge trembled as the train sped closer and closer.

Duchess and O'Malley covered the children with their bodies. The kittens closed their eyes and covered their ears as the smoking train thundered overhead.

TOOOT-TOOOOOOOOOOOOOOT!

The cats clung to the shaking trestle with all their might. But as the train roared into the distance, they heard a splash.

Duchess screamed. Marie had fallen into the river!

CHAPTER EIGHT

O'Malley, like most cats, detested getting wet.
But he didn't even think about that now as he
dived into the river to save Marie.

Moments later he held the kitten by his
teeth as he grabbed on to a bobbing log. But
the water's strong current was carrying the
log downriver.

Duchess had leaped down from the
bridge. Now she raced along the river's edge
until she found a tree whose low-hanging

branch reached out over the water. She clambered out to the end of the branch, her eyes fixed on the pair in the water.

"Thomas!" Duchess shouted.

At just the right moment O'Malley tossed Marie into the air.

Duchess reached out and caught her daughter. Then she carried the soaked and sobbing kitten to the ground.

Duchess licked at Marie's wet fur and hugged her tightly, then glanced back at the river. O'Malley still clung to the log as it was swept along by the swirling waters.

"Thomas!"

"I'm all right, honey," O'Malley called out. "Don't worry. I'll see you downstream!"

Two British geese—twin sisters named Amelia and Abigail Gabble—just happened to be walking along the riverbank at that very moment.

"I say," Abigail said to Amelia. "Look over there."

"Oh!" squawked Amelia. "How unusual!"

They stood and watched for a moment as O'Malley tried desperately to swim to shore, gasping and choking in the fierce current.

"Fancy that," Abigail said. "A cat learning how to swim."

Amelia shook her head. "Oh, but he's going about it all the wrong way."

"Quite," Abigail agreed. "We must correct him."

Full of good intentions, the twin geese paddled out into the river to give O'Malley some quick swimming lessons. But what was second nature to the geese was not so simple for a cat. By the time the twins got through with him, O'Malley was nearly drowned.

But at last they pulled the sputtering cat to the edge of the river.

"You really did quite well for a beginner," Abigail pronounced encouragingly. "Just keep practicing!"

Dripping and coughing up water, O'Malley glared at the geese as Duchess and the kittens surrounded him.

"Oh, Thomas!" Duchess said. "Thank goodness you're safe."

"Can I help you, Monsieur O'Malley?"

Toulouse asked.

"No, thanks," O'Malley muttered. "I've had all the help I can take."

Introductions were made. Abigail and Amelia Gabble were on holiday, taking a walking tour of France. As it turned out, they were on their way to Paris, too.

"We're going to meet Uncle Waldo at Le Petit Café," Abigail explained.

"The famous restaurant?" Duchess exclaimed. *"C'est magnifique!"*

"Why don't you join us?" Amelia asked.

"I think that's a wonderful idea," Duchess agreed.

"Oh, no . . ." O'Malley groaned. He had quite enough of the geese's company for one day.

But the others ignored him. Amelia and Abigail lined up the kittens in the shape of a V, the way geese fly in the sky when they fly south for the winter. Duchess and O'Malley took their places at the rear.

"Now," said Abigail. "Think goose! Forward *march*!" Proudly she led the way toward Paris.

"Mama," whispered Berlioz. "Do we have

to waddle like they do?"

"Yes, dear," replied Duchess quietly. "It's the polite thing to do."

By the time the odd group of travelers reached the outskirts of Paris, the sun had set and the streetlights had been lit. At last they reached Le Petit Café and found Uncle Waldo hanging on to a lampost just outside the elegant restaurant. The old goose had just escaped from the kitchen. His hat was on crooked, and he had a serious case of the hiccups. In fact, Uncle Waldo was quite drunk.

Abigail and Amelia were shocked. But when Uncle Waldo pointed at the menu posted in the window, they understood. Listed as the special of the day was Prime Country Goose à la Provençal, stuffed with chestnuts and basted in white wine. Before his narrow escape from the kitchen, poor Uncle Waldo had been doused in wine by the chef of Le Petit Café.

"Abigail," whispered Amelia. "We'd best get Uncle Waldo to bed."

The three geese said farewell to their new feline friends and waddled off down the cobblestone street.

O'Malley and Duchess set their sights on the Eiffel Tower and continued their journey through the dark winding streets of Paris. But it was getting late, and the children were quickly growing weary. O'Malley carried Marie on his back as they stole across the rooftops of the city.

"Mama," Marie whimpered. "I'm so tired."

"Me, too," Berlioz complained. "My feet hurt."

"I bet we walked a hundred miles today," Toulouse added.

"Look, baby," O'Malley told Duchess. "It's late and the kids are bushed. I know a place where you can stay the night. It's just around that next chimney pot."

Duchess was worried about Madame. "Are you sure we can't get home tonight?"

O'Malley shook his head. He pointed toward the attic of an old run-down house. Soft light glowed through the skylight. "It's not exactly the Ritz," O'Malley said as he led the way. "But it's peaceful and quiet and you'll—"

Music blared from inside as O'Malley opened the window.

The kittens perked up immediately. This music was different from the elegant classical piano music they were used to. This music was rowdy and noisy and fun, with a beat that seemed to enter their bones and make their feet want to dance. It filled the dark night with magic and excitement.

O'Malley winced. "Oh, no." He smiled apologetically at Duchess. "Sounds like my buddy Scat Cat and his gang have dropped by."

Duchess tried to hide her smile. "Friends of yours?"

"Uh-huh. Old buddies of mine. But they're, uh, not exactly your type, Duchess. Maybe we'd better find another place, huh?"

"No, no," Duchess insisted. "This will be fine, I'm sure. I'd like to meet your Scat Cat."

O'Malley shrugged. "Well, okay." He cupped his hands and shouted down into the room. "Hey, Scat Cat, blow some of that sweet music my way."

A fat gray cat in a red bow tie put down his trumpet and laughed. "Well, lookie here!

Big Man O'Malley is back in his alley. Swing on down here, daddy!"

O'Malley jumped down into the room. He and Scat Cat smacked paws.

Then O'Malley introduced Duchess to Scat Cat and the rest of the gang, five cats of all shapes and sizes who had been playing the guitar, the bass, the piano, the concertina, and the drums.

Duchess held up her paw. "I'm delighted to meet you, Monsieur Scat Cat."

Scat Cat removed his hat and kissed her paw. "Likewise, Duchess. You're too much."

"And your music. . ." Duchess went on. "It's so . . . different, so exciting."

By then Berlioz had found his way to the piano and began to play, imitating the new music he'd just heard.

"Say," said Scat Cat, leaning on the piano. "This kitty cat knows where it's at."

Scat Cat and his friends grabbed their instruments and picked up the beat, and soon the room was swinging. Duchess and O'Malley danced around the room as the kittens joined in with the band.

When she got tired of dancing, Duchess

sat down and played a solo on the harp that was sitting in one corner of the room. O'Malley gazed at her in surprise. Why, this dame had beauty, brains, guts—and talent to boot. By the time Duchess finished her song, the alley cat was a goner. For the first time ever, O'Malley the alley cat was completely and hopelessly in love.

It was late when Scat Cat and his pals finally said good night. Duchess tucked her worn-out kittens into bed and kissed them. "Happy dreams, my loves," she whispered.

Then she joined O'Malley on the windowsill.

"I bet they're on that magic carpet right now," he said with a grin.

Duchess laughed softly. "They could hardly keep their eyes open! Such an exciting day."

"It sure was," O'Malley agreed. "And what a finale!"

"Thomas, your friends are really delightful," Duchess said. "I just love them."

"Well, they're a little rough around the edges," O'Malley admitted, leaping off the windowsill onto a nearby roof ledge. "But if you're ever in a jam—wham! They're right there."

Duchess followed O'Malley to the ledge, smiling up at him with shining eyes. "And when we needed you, you were right there, too."

O'Malley blushed. "Hey, that was just a lucky break . . . for me."

They gazed into the starry night for a while, at the Eiffel Tower, at the beautiful skyline of Paris. They didn't notice when the kittens sat up in bed, then crept to the windowsill to spy.

"And those little kittens . . . I sure love 'em, Duchess," O'Malley admitted.

"And they are very fond of you," Duchess replied.

O'Malley cleared his throat. "Yeah, well, you know . . . they really need a . . . a father around."

The kittens gasped in delight. Berlioz and Toulouse started giggling, but Marie quickly shushed her brothers. She wanted to hear every word.

"Oh, Thomas," Duchess replied, "that would be wonderful. If only I could stay here with you. . . ."

"Why can't you?" O'Malley asked, surprised. He had been sure that Duchess felt the same way about him that he felt about her.

Duchess turned away. "Because of Madame. I . . . I could never leave her."

O'Malley looked stunned. "But Madame's just a human. You're just house pets to her!"

"No," Duchess insisted. "We mean far more to her than that." Duchess sighed at the crushed look on O'Malley's face. She didn't wish to hurt him. She had grown so fond of this brave, rascally alley cat. But she could tell he just didn't understand about Madame. "I'm sorry, my dear. But we must go home tomorrow."

O'Malley shrugged and looked away. "Yeah, well, I guess you know best," he said softly. "But I'm sure gonna miss you . . . and those kids."

Marie sighed.

Toulouse punched his pillow in disappointment.

"Shoot," Berlioz said. "We *almost* had a father."

CHAPTER NINE

Roquefort perched on the windowsill of Madame's room the next morning and gazed sadly into the quiet street. He could think of nothing but Duchess and the kittens. Would he ever see them again?

He could almost picture them right now playing happily around the piano . . . sharing their dinner with him . . . running along the cobblestone streets toward the mansion . . .

Roquefort jumped up. He pressed his nose to the glass and stared into the street. It was them! It was really them!

"Duchess! Kittens!" he cried. "They're back!" Quickly he slid down the curtains and scurried down the stairs toward the front door.

But when he passed the front parlor, he skidded to a stop on the polished marble floor. He had just spotted Edgar sitting in an overstuffed armchair with a bottle of champagne.

"Edgar!" Roquefort cried in dismay. He had almost forgotten all about the scheming butler. If Edgar saw the cats returning he was sure to do something desperate. Thinking fast, the little mouse scurried over to the butler's shoes and tied his shoelaces together.

Edgar held up the bottle of champagne. "Edgar, you sly old fox," he said to himself, "it's time to get used to the finer things in life. After all, someday they're all going to be yours." He popped the cork on the champagne bottle.

The cork hit Roquefort in the tummy

and sent him flying against the wall.

Edgar didn't notice. Raising his glass, the butler made a toast. "To the good life!" he exclaimed. He took a sip of champagne.

Scratch! Scratch! Scratch!

"Meow! Meow! Meow!"

The startled Edgar spewed out the mouthful of champagne. "No!" he gasped. "It can't be them!" He jumped up to run to the door. But he tripped on his tied shoelaces and tumbled to the floor with a crash.

Roquefort dashed to the front door. He had to warn the cats. He tried to push through the kitty door, but it wouldn't budge. It was locked!

Frantic, Roquefort climbed up to the front windowsill and waved his arms at Duchess and the kittens. "Don't come in!" he squeaked as loudly as he could.

Toulouse saw him and smiled. "Look—there's Roquefort!"

The kittens thought Roquefort was waving to them. So they waved back.

Roquefort waved harder. He jumped up and down, shouting, "Go away! GO AWAY!"

But the cats couldn't hear his tiny voice through the glass.

"Boy," said Berlioz. "He sure is glad to see us!"

Duchess frowned. Odd . . . Madame never locked the kitty door. While they waited for Edgar to open the door, Duchess and O'Malley said their good-byes.

"I don't know what to say," Duchess said. "I only wish—"

"Hey," O'Malley said with a shrug, doing his best to hide his sadness. "Maybe just a short, sweet good-bye would be the easiest."

Duchess blinked back a tear. "I'll never forget you, Thomas O'Malley."

O'Malley tried to smile as he said, "So long, baby." Then he hurried off down the street.

The front door swung open. Edgar had finally managed to untie his shoelaces and get up.

"Duchess!" Edgar said, pretending to be surprised and delighted. "Wherever have you been?"

"Don't come in!" Roquefort shouted one

71

last time. But Duchess and her kittens were so happy to be home that they had already rushed inside.

Edgar slammed the door.

Down the block O'Malley stopped and turned around. He stared up at the stately mansion with its butler and its beautiful gardens. Wow! he thought. He'd known Duchess was a high-class lady. But he'd never dreamed she came from a home as grand as this. No wonder she had been so anxious to get back. In a house like that, the cats probably got cream for dinner every night.

"Well, they're home safe and sound," he told himself. "I guess they won't need me anymore."

With a sad lump in his throat, O'Malley the alley cat turned and headed back toward the poor part of town.

CHAPTER TEN

But things were not what they seemed behind the closed door of the mansion.

Duchess and her kittens were not safe and sound.

A frantic Roquefort slid down the curtain, shouting, "Duchess! Watch out for the—"

But his warning came too late. Edgar had already scooped up the cats in a canvas sack. He tied a knot and pulled it tight.

"sack . . ." Roquefort finished dejectedly.

Edgar held up the sack of squirming, clawing cats. "You came back!" Edgar fumed. "It just isn't fair!" He had to get rid of these pesky animals once and for all, before they ruined everything for him.

"Edgar!" Madame shouted from upstairs. "Edgar! Come quickly!"

Edgar whirled around. "Uh—coming, Madame," he called. The sack—he had to hide it! But where?

Thinking quickly, he dashed to the kitchen and yanked open the oven door. Then he stuffed the sack full of cats inside. "I'll take care of you later," he hissed.

He shrugged into his suit coat as he hurried into the front hall.

Madame Bonfamille flew down the stairs. "Oh, Edgar!" she cried with a hopeful smile on her face. "They're back. I heard them!"

Edgar buttoned his jacket and walked calmly toward the front door.

"Hurry!" Madame insisted as she followed him. "Let them in!"

Edgar opened the door. The front porch was empty.

Surprised, Madame lifted her long skirts and hurried down the steps. "Duchess! Kittens! Come here, my darlings. Where are you?"

Edgar stepped out onto the porch. "Allow me, Madame." He cleared his throat. "Here, kitty, kitty, kitty. Here, kitty, kitty."

Meanwhile, Roquefort had slipped into the kitchen. He stood on the oven handle and listened as Duchess whispered to him through the oven door.

Roquefort scratched his head. "His name is O'What?"

"O'Malley," Duchess repeated patiently. The little mouse could be their only chance for freedom. She wanted to be sure he had it right.

Marie added, "Abraham de Lacy Giuseppe Casey—"

"Oh, never mind!" Duchess said. "Just run, Roquefort. Go get him. And please hurry!"

The little mouse jumped to the floor. "I'm on my way!"

Now all the cats could do was wait. Inside the sack Toulouse grumbled, "I *told* you it was Edgar."

Minutes ticked by slowly. It was dark inside the sack and hard to breathe. The kittens squirmed. Duchess held her breath and listened. At last they all heard the front door slam. Then they heard Edgar and Madame talking in the front hall.

"Oh, it's no use, Edgar," Madame said sadly. "I'm afraid it was just the imagination of a lonely old lady." She turned toward the stairs, shaking her head. "But I was so sure that I heard them. . . ."

Edgar did his best to look sad. "I'm so sorry, Madame."

Inside the oven, Duchess and her kittens called out to their mistress, meowing as loudly as they could from inside the heavy sack.

But it was too late. Madame had hurried up the stairs to her room and shut the door.

Duchess hugged her kittens tightly. But she dared not say what she was thinking.

Madame would never hear them now.

CHAPTER ELEVEN

Roquefort scampered into the street in front of Madame Bonfamille's mansion. Which way? *Which way?*

Down the block he caught a glimpse of a white-tipped tail as it disappeared around the corner of a redbrick building.

Roquefort dashed after it. He turned the corner and spotted the cat. It was him—the alley cat Roquefort had seen with Duchess. Gasping for breath, Roquefort bravely ran out in front of him and shouted, "Hey! Stop!"

O'Malley stared curiously at the little gray mouse in the brown hat and coat, but he kept walking. Normally he would have pounced immediately—a nice plump mouse made a fine snack. But right now he was too depressed to bother.

"Duchess . . . kittens . . . in trouble!" Roquefort gasped. "Butler did it!" he added.

O'Malley stopped in his tracks. "Duchess and the kittens are in trouble?"

The little mouse nodded, trying to catch his breath.

"Look," O'Malley said urgently. "You go get Scat Cat and his gang of alley cats."

"Alley cats?" Roquefort gulped. "But I'm a mouse!"

"Hey," O'Malley said, "I'm gonna need help."

Roquefort's knees started knocking. "You mean you want me—"

"Move!" O'Malley ordered as he turned and raced back toward the mansion. "Just tell 'em O'Malley sent you. You won't have a bit of trouble."

Roquefort trembled with fear. But he

knew he had to help Duchess and the kittens. Still shaking, he ran off in the direction O'Malley had been heading. Street by street, the little mouse began the search, running along the cluttered, twisting back alleys of Paris as fast as his tiny feet could take him.

"No trouble, he said," Roquefort muttered as he searched. "That's easy for . . . old what's-his-name to say. He's got *nine* lives. I've only got one."

Suddenly Roquefort was running, but he wasn't going anywhere. His feet lifted off the ground. Someone had grabbed him by the tail.

He rose in the air until he dangled inches from the sharp teeth of a big gray cat in a red bow tie. "What's a little swinger like you doin' on our side of town?" the cat asked with a laugh. It was Scat Cat.

"Oh, please," Roquefort begged. "I was sent here for help . . . by a cat!"

Scat Cat and his pals hooted with laughter.

"Honest," Roquefort insisted. "He told me just to mention his name."

Scat Cat dropped the mouse into another cat's hand.

"So start mentioning names," the second cat suggested.

Roquefort was so terrified that he couldn't think straight. "Now, wait a minute. . . . D-don't rush me. His name is . . . O'Toole."

"Strike one," Scat Cat sneered.

"No, wait—O'Brien!"

"Strike two!" Scat Cat cheered.

Roquefort gulped. "Oh, boy. How about . . . O'Grady?"

"Mousey," Scat Cat announced, "you just struck out. Any last words?"

Trembling, Roquefort closed his eyes. "Oh, why did I ever listen to that O'Malley cat?" he squeaked.

"O'Malley?" Scat Cat exclaimed. "Hold it, cats! This little guy is on the level."

"Sorry, Squeaky," said one of the other cats. "We didn't mean to rough you up."

"Don't worry about me," Roquefort said, sighing with relief. "O'Malley needs help. Duchess and the kittens are in trouble!"

Scat Cat gasped. "Duchess and the kittens? Come on, cats, we gotta split." He and his pals took off down the street.

"Wait for me!" Roquefort cried, chasing

after the cats. "You don't know the way!"

Nearby, a man having lunch at a corner café stared in amazement. One tiny gray mouse was chasing a whole gang of worried-looking cats down the street.

The man rubbed his eyes, shook his head, and poured out his wine into a flowerpot.

CHAPTER TWELVE

J. Thomas O'Malley peeked into the windows
of Madame Bonfamille's mansion one by one.
At last he spotted Edgar. The butler was talking
on the telephone and holding a squirming sack.

A wave of anger washed over O'Malley.
No human was going to hurt Duchess and her
kittens as long as he was around!

Edgar smiled as he hung up the phone
and left the room with the sack.

O'Malley hurried to the back of the

house just in time to spot Edgar dashing into the barn. The alley cat ran to the barn and jumped up to an open window. He looked inside and saw Edgar dumping the squirming bag of cats into a large trunk.

"Now, my pesky little pets," Edgar said, "you're going to travel first class—in your own private compartment." Smiling, the butler slammed the lid and clicked the combination lock into place. "All the way to Timbuktu," Edgar finished. "And this time you'll *never* come back!"

O'Malley slipped in through the window to the hayloft as Edgar pushed the heavy trunk toward the door. "We've got . . . to hurry," he grunted. "The baggage truck . . . *umph!* . . . will be here any moment now."

O'Malley waited until Edgar was right below him, then—

"*MEOWWWW!*" With an ear-splitting howl, O'Malley dived onto Edgar's shoulders, sending him sprawling across the trunk.

Edgar was stunned, but only for a moment. Angrily he jumped up and started chasing O'Malley. Frou-Frou the horse jumped forward and grabbed the butler's coattails in her teeth. But Edgar pulled free and threw a pitchfork straight at O'Malley. Frou-Frou whinnied a warning. O'Malley ducked just in time to avoid the deadly prongs. But, they landed in the wall on either side of him—he was trapped!

Edgar laughed out loud, then turned back to his work. He ran to the barn door and flung it open . . .

Scat Cat and his pals waved hello to the surprised butler, then jumped on him, scratching, clawing, and hissing for all they were worth.

Roquefort saw his chance. He crawled onto the lid of the trunk and spun the dial of the combination lock.

By the time the lock clicked open, O'Malley had worked his way free of the pitchfork. He flung open the trunk, jumped inside, and struggled to untie the sack. "Everybody out of here—fast!" he urged Duchess and the kittens.

But Edgar had escaped from Scat Cat's gang and snuck up on the trunk. He slammed the lid shut before O'Malley and the others could escape. "You're *all* going to Timbuktu—

if it's the last thing I do!" Edgar shouted. He jumped on top of the trunk, swinging a club to keep Scat Cat and his gang away.

Two of the cats left the group and scampered up to the hayloft. They picked up a leather horse collar, dragged it to the edge of the loft, and dropped it on Edgar. Before he knew what had hit him, the butler's arms were pinned to his side by the heavy collar.

Scat Cat threw a bucket of water at Edgar, and the pail landed on the butler's head like a hat that was too big. Another cat jumped forward, hooked a pulley to the horse collar, and gave Frou-Frou a signal.

Frou-Frou pulled the rope, which raised Edgar off the trunk. O'Malley, Duchess, and the kittens jumped out.

Then, with one swift kick, Frou-Frou sent Edgar flying into the trunk. The force of the horse's kick slammed the lid shut and sent the trunk sliding out of the barn . . .

. . . just as the baggage truck backed up to the door.

The driver leaned over and peered at the label. "Well, this must be the trunk."

"Yup," said the driver's assistant. "And

she goes all the way to Timbuktu." The two men heaved the heavy trunk onto the back of the truck, then locked the door.

"Fffft! Ffffft!" Toulouse hissed, arching his back and baring his claws as the truck drove away. He was glad Edgar had gotten what he deserved. He only wished he'd been able to help more during the big fight—just like a tough alley cat.

Duchess gazed at the truck until it disappeared. She sighed, then turned to hug her children tight.

CHAPTER THIRTEEN

That night Monsieur Georges Hautecourt arrived at Madame Bonfamille's mansion.

But Madame was in too happy a mood to think about her lawyer's paperwork. Duchess and the kittens were home!

Monsieur Hautecourt watched in amusement as Madame posed Duchess, the kittens, and a large, rather dashingly handsome alley cat on a love seat. She had brought out a big black camera so she could take a photograph of them. Why, she'd even dressed up the new cat in a white collar and bright green bow tie.

"Now, my pets," Madame instructed. "Move a little closer together. Good! Look, Georges. What do you think?"

"Very good, very good!" The old lawyer chuckled affectionately. It was wonderful to see his dear Adelaide with that sparkle in her eyes again. "But I think we should get on with the will."

Madame waved an impatient hand. "Yes, yes, of course. But you know what to do."

The lawyer sat down at the desk, put his reading glasses back on his nose, and picked up his pen. "Very well." He made a sweeping slash mark on his paper. "Scratch one butler."

"You know, Georges," Madame said as she adjusted the focus on the camera, "if Edgar had only known about the will, I'm sure he would never have left." Poor Madame had no idea what had happened to her faithful servant. But in her joy over having her beloved cats back, she didn't think about it very much. She could get a new butler.

Duchess and the kittens were irreplaceable.

Madame stood back and studied her subjects. Then she bustled to her dressing table for a comb.

"Duchess, it's wonderful to have you all back," she said as she crossed to the love seat. She combed O'Malley's hair a bit. "And I think this young man is very handsome." She winked at Duchess. "Shall we keep him in the family?"

Toulouse, Berlioz, and Marie answered at once: *"Meow!"*

Duchess smiled up at O'Malley and purred. Although her human mistress couldn't understand the words, the beautiful white cat's sparkling sapphire eyes held all the answer Madame needed.

"Of course we will," Madame said with a smile. "We need a man around the house!" She hurried back to her camera and looked through the lens. "Now—don't move. Smile. And say cheese!"

Roquefort poked his nose out of his mouse hole. "Did somebody say cheese?" he squeaked.

Madame snapped the picture. "Wonderful!

Thank you. Now, my dears," she added with a secret smile, "run along downstairs. There's a surprise for you."

Madame opened the door, and music flooded the room. Roquefort grabbed on to Toulouse's tail as the cats ran for the stairs.

"Adelaide!" cried Monsieur Hautecourt. "What's that music?" He jumped up from the desk and danced a few steps. "Sounds like a gang of swinging hepcats!"

"That's exactly what they are," Madame said, swaying to the jazz music. "They're the start of my new foundation."

"What foundation?" asked Monsieur Hautecourt.

Madame led him to the top of the stairs and pointed toward the parlor. "My home for all the homeless alley cats of Paris!"

The house was swarming with cats of every size, shape, and color. Scat Cat and his gang were playing music—music that was rowdy and noisy and fun. Music with a beat that got right into your bones and made your feet want to dance. Music that filled the many empty rooms of the mansion with magic and excitement.

Duchess and O'Malley laughed in delight as Toulouse, Berlioz, and Marie ran to the piano to join in the fun.

O'Malley grinned. Maybe Duchess was right. Maybe some humans were okay after all—especially Madame Adelaide Bonfamille. Anybody who loved cats the way she did couldn't be all bad!

As the music continued, O'Malley gave Duchess a wink and swept her into his arms.

Oh! thought Duchess joyfully as they danced across the room. Aristocats and alley cats—what lucky cats we are!

About the Movie

The Aristocats was originally planned as a television special that would star *real* cats, but Walt Disney decided that he wanted to make it into an animated film. The artists and writers began working on the film in 1963, and it wasn't finished until 1970! Walt Disney approved all the plans for the film in 1966, just months before his death. In fact, *The Aristocats* was the last animated feature Walt Disney was involved with.

The Aristocats is among the twenty top-grossing animated films of all times. It was such a success during its initial run in movie theaters that it was rereleased in 1980 and again in 1987.